Cover and page design by Luis C. Lewis - Big Red Balloon Copyright 2014

Luis C. Lewis's

Liam, Are You Sleepy Yet?

Liam, are you sleepy yet?

Nope.

Aren't you tired from a full day of pretending?

Nope.

Aren't you exhausted
from all your battles?

Nope.

Aren't you worn out from your wild chases?

Nope.

But Liam, aren't you beat from your amazing feuds?

Nope.

Doesn't snuggling up with
a blanket sound comfy?

Nope.

Doesn't resting on a big soft pillow sound great?

Nope.

Are you sure you're not even a bit sleepy?

Liam?

Let's remove your beanie and get you comfortable.

Oh that's right... You hate morning bed head.

But you're feeling sleepy now, aren't you?

Nope.

You know you can dream of your adventures, right?

And tomorrow you can pretend all over again.

So are you sleepy now?

Yuuuuup.

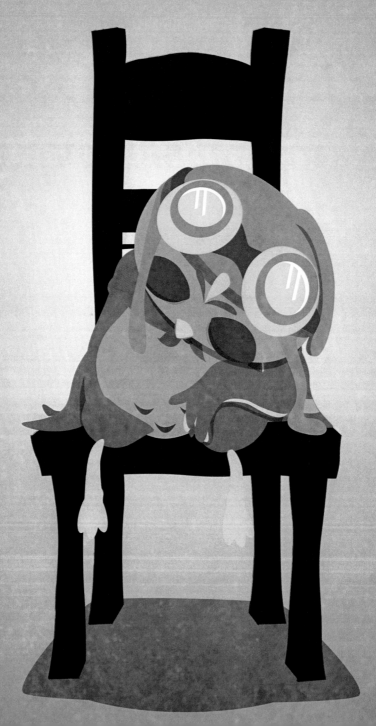